Who Will Ask THE FOUR QUESTIONS?

'To Grandpa Oded, we all miss you so much.'
NBG

'For Eve Joyce Lwando.'
TTT

Green Bean Books

First published in the UK in 2020 by Green Bean Books
c/o Pen & Sword Books Ltd
47 Church Street, Barnsley, S. Yorkshire, S70 2AS
www.greenbeanbooks.com

Text © Naomi Ben-Gur, 2018
Illustrations © Carmel Ben-Ami, 2018
Copyright © Hakibbutz-Hameuchad Ltd, 2018
English language translation © Harold Grinspoon Foundation
English edition © Green Bean Books, 2020

Paperback edition: 978-1-78438-463-0
Harold Grinspoon Foundation edition: 978-1-78438-467-8

Designed by Tina García
Edited by Kate Baker, Claire Berliner, Julie Carpenter and Phoebe Jascourt
Production by Hugh Allan

Printed in China by Imago
032032K1/B1484/A5

MIX
Paper from
responsible sources
FSC® C016973

Who Will Ask THE FOUR QUESTIONS?

Written by **Naomi Ben-Gur**   Illustrated by **Carmel Ben-Ami**

Translated by **Gilah Kahn-Hoffmann**

"Grandma Naomi, look at the guitar that Mum bought for me!"

I ran to my room, picked up my new guitar, and started to play.

"You sound like a real pop star," she beamed.

"This is how I'll sing the Four Questions – Ma Nishtana – on seder night," I said. Grandma was delighted.

"You were so wonderful last year!"

But then we heard a voice from the corner of the room.

"No, it's my turn this year! *I'm going to sing!*"

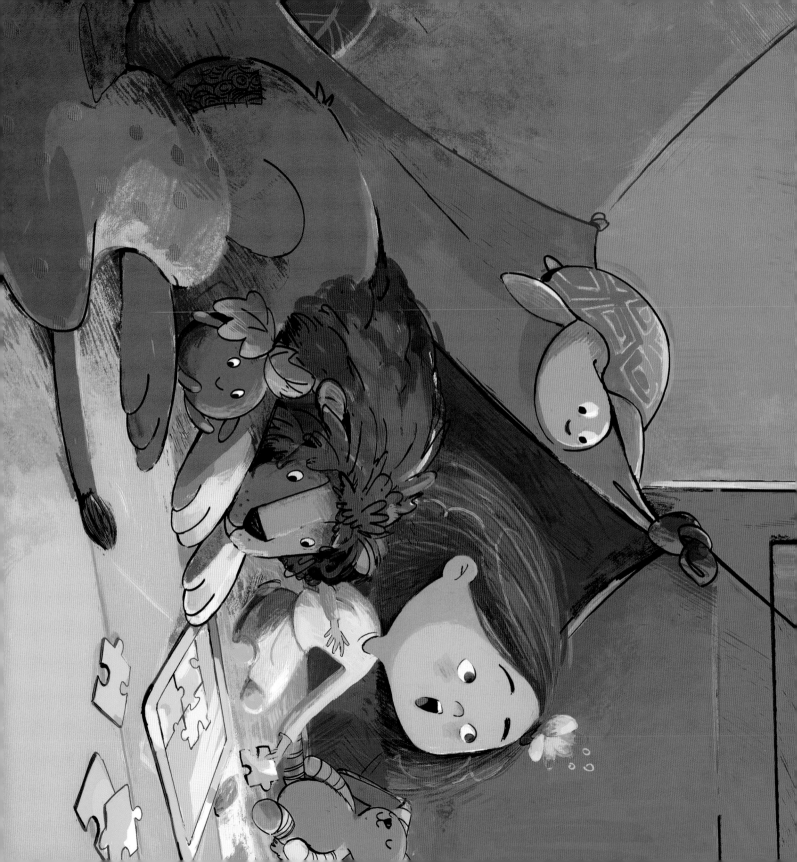

I looked over at my little sister Evie, who was doing a puzzle.

"I'm going to sing Ma Mishtana this year," she said again.

"It's not Ma **M**ishtana, it's Ma **N**ishtana, with an N," I told her.

"See! You're too young. You can't get the words right!"

"I can!" Evie insisted.

"Why don't you sing together?"
suggested Grandma.
"No," Evie protested,
"I can sing by myself!"

"My teacher said that the
youngest always sings
Ma Mishtana."

"You're still getting it wrong,"
I laughed. But Evie insisted,
"I do know it – I just got
a little confused."

"I *am* old enough and
I *can* do it. Grandma,
will you teach me?"

Grandma stroked my head.

"Eitan, sweetheart,
you're Evie's big brother.

Maybe you could teach her
to sing the Four Questions?"

"I don't want to," I complained.

"Can't she just sing next year?"

But Evie wasn't giving up that easily.

"I'm the littlest, so I'm going to sing
this year."

The next time Grandma Naomi came to visit, she took Evie into Mum and Dad's bedroom. When I pressed my ear to the door, I heard Grandma teaching her to sing the Four Questions.

"Ma Mishtana..." Evie began.

"Oh Grandma," she cried, "I still can't get it right!"

"Don't worry," Grandma said. "You're allowed to get mixed up. Grown-ups get mixed up too."

When I complained to Mum and Dad, they told me I had to let Evie sing.

"It's not fair!" I stamped my feet. "What will I do instead?"

"You could recite the Ten Plagues," Dad suggested.

"I don't want to," I moaned. "I want to sing the Four Questions!"

I had one final idea. One evening, when we were going to bed, I asked Evie softly, "Do you want my new guitar?"

"Yes!" she exclaimed.

"You can have it if you let me sing the Four Questions."

She hugged her blankie and didn't say a word.

"Okay?" I asked, wishing that she would say yes.

"No," she said at last, in a small voice.

Seder night finally arrived. Evie and I helped to get everything ready. I put out the napkins on one side of the table, and Evie set the other side. Hers were a little crooked. I wanted to straighten them out for her, but she got upset.

When the guests arrived, they went straight to the kitchen, carrying pots, baskets, and trays. There was wine for the grown-ups and sweet grape juice for the children. *I'll drink four glasses of that later!* I thought.

Auntie Jenia brought nut cake. Grandpa Avi brought fish. Auntie Netta brought hot soup with matzah balls – Evie's favourite!

Everyone took turns reading from the Haggadah. "And now," Mum smiled at Evie, "we'll hear Ma Nishtana."

The room fell silent as Evie stood on her chair. She looked nervous. She glanced at our aunts and uncles and cousins, and then stared at me. Maybe she would finally give in and let me sing?

I moved my lips soundlessly around the words "Ma Nishtana". Suddenly – I don't know how it happened – I heard myself sing those first two words. Evie then continued in her own voice, loud and clear . . .

מַה נִּשְׁתַּנָּה הַלַּיְלָה הַזֶּה מִכָּל הַלֵּילוֹת

"Ha-laylah ha-zeh, mi-kol ha-leylot." And so it went on. I started each question by singing "Ma Nishtana," and Evie followed. She sang all Four Questions. When she was finished, everyone cheered. "Wonderful, Evie!" "Fantastic!"

I joined in, brimming with pride.

"Just a minute," Grandma Naomi called out.
"Let's not forget to thank Eitan for helping Evie so nicely.
Tonight you showed us all what a fantastic big brother
you are!" Everyone clapped. But strongest of all clapped
Evie, my not-so-little sister.

The Story of Passover

The first Passover happened long ago in the far-away country of Egypt. A mean and powerful king, called Pharaoh, ruled Egypt. Worried that the Jewish people would one day fight against him, Pharaoh decided that these people must become his slaves. As slaves, the Jewish people worked very hard. Every day, from morning until night, they hammered, dug, and carried heavy bricks. They built palaces and cities and worked without rest. The Jewish people hated being slaves. They cried and asked God for help. God chose a man named Moses to lead the Jewish people. Moses went to Pharaoh and said, "God is not happy with the way you treat the Jewish people. He wants you to let the Jewish people leave Egypt and go into the desert, where they will be free." But Pharaoh stamped his foot and shouted, "No, I will never let the Jewish people go!" Moses warned, "If you do not listen to God, many terrible things, called plagues, will come to your land." But Pharaoh would not listen, and so the plagues arrived. First, the water turned to blood. Next, frogs and, later, wild animals ran in and out of homes. Balls of hail fell from the sky and bugs, called locusts, ate all of the Egyptians' food.

Each time a new plague began, Pharaoh would cry, "Moses, I'll let the Jewish people go. Just stop this horrible plague!" Yet no sooner would God take away the plague than Pharaoh would shout: "No, I've changed my mind. The Jews must stay!" So God sent more plagues. Finally, as the tenth plague arrived, Pharaoh ordered the Jews to leave Egypt.

Fearful that Pharaoh might again change his mind, the Jewish people packed quickly. They had no time to prepare food and no time to allow their dough to rise into puffy bread. They had only enough time to make a flat, cracker-like bread called matzah. They hastily tied the matzah to their backs and ran from their homes.

The people had not travelled far before Pharaoh commanded his army to chase after them and bring them back to Egypt. The Jews dashed forward, but stopped when they reached a large sea. The sea was too big to swim across. Frightened that Pharaoh's men would soon reach them, the people prayed to God, and a miracle occurred. The sea opened up. Two walls of water stood in front of them and a dry, sandy path stretched between the walls. The Jews ran across. Just as they reached the other side, the walls of water fell and the path disappeared. The sea now separated the Jews from the land of Egypt. They were free!

Each year at Passover, we eat special foods, sing songs, tell stories, and participate in a seder — a special meal designed to help us remember this miraculous journey from slavery to freedom.

Engaging Children with Passover

Here are some suggestions to make Passover memorable and fun for your children. (Remember, there's no one right way to celebrate the holiday.)

★ First, be prepared to enjoy Passover. Your children will react to your mood of pleasure and playfulness.

★ Traditionally, the person leading the seder reclines on a pillow to signify the ease of being a free person. Anyone who chooses can have such a pillow. Encourage your children to use paint or fabric pens to give a Passover theme to a plain pillowcase. At the seder, be sure to give credit for the fabulous results.

★ Recipes fascinate some children. Let your children help choose a new food to introduce at the seder. *Charoset*, the fragrant mixture symbolic of the mortar used by the Hebrew slaves, lends itself especially well to variations.

★ A Passover play may be in your future. In advance of the holiday, encourage your children to choose a portion of the Passover story and act it out with siblings and/or friends. Help them get creative with costumes and props. Their play might even be presented at the seder!

★ Consider having a child's version of a *Haggadah* (the text used by seder participants) at the seder.

★ Give all children who are able a chance to read a few sentences from it. Be sure to let them rehearse in advance so they'll feel comfortable.

★ Encourage the important Jewish tradition of asking questions. As the seder begins, inform everyone that Uncle Max (or Grandma Rose) has a small treat for any child who asks a Passover question.

★ Vary the songs at the seder. Perhaps your children learn Passover songs at school, or you could check online for simple songs with familiar tunes.

★ During the seder, ask everyone present to close her or his eyes, picture what freedom looks like, and give a one-word description. As an alternative, ask each person to name something wonderful that happened in the past year.

★ Jewish holidays are important times to think of others. In this spirit, when shopping for Passover groceries, encourage your children to choose an item to give to a local food bank or homeless shelter.